the clumsy elf

©2021 melissa spencer

www.merryelfmas.com

You may also like...

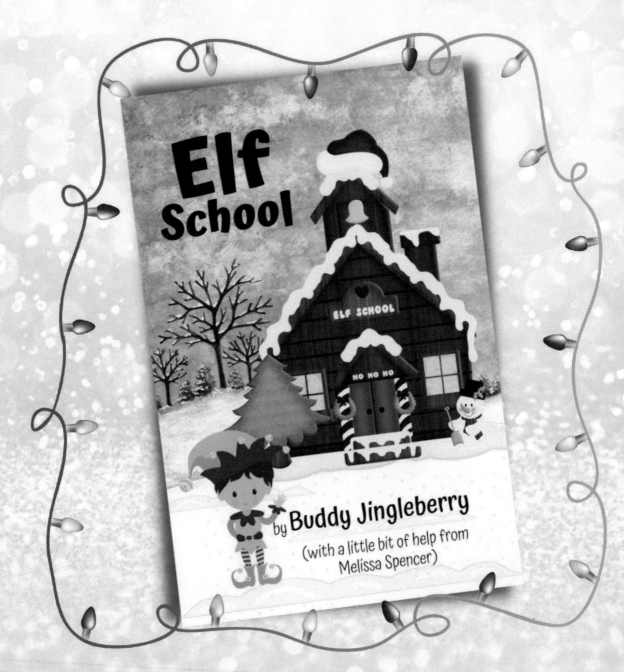

Elf School

by Buddy Jingleberry

(with a little bit of help from Melissa Spencer)

Trip was a kind elf who always
made everyone laugh
in Santa's Village.

North Pole

Sadly, they all laughed AT him because he was so clumsy. Whenever anything went wrong in Santa's Workshop, he was always in the middle of the muddle.

One day, Santa asked Trip to help decorate the Christmas tree. 'Maybe you will be a bit more... you know, a little less...' said Santa.

But Trip got all the tinsel in a tangle.

Instead Trip helped look after the reindeer.
As he climbed on Prancer's back to brush him,
a fly landed on Trip's hand.
'Hello fly!' laughed Trip.

Prancer only heard
the word
FLY!

They shot up in the air,
leaving a twinkling trail!

In a panic, Trip called
'Dancer! Down!'
Onwards they flew,
higher and higher.
'Plaster! Down!'
he shouted. They flew
faster and faster.
'Disaster!' he yelled.

When exhausted Prancer finally flew back to the stables, Santa was waiting. 'Trip, don't worry,' said Santa. 'Just be ready to leave in the morning.'

uh oh! I'm in trouble.
I'm such a clumsy elf, I can't do anything right.

All I want is to make Santa proud,
and now he's sending me away.

The next morning, Santa gave Trip a letter addressed to Tim. With a wink, Santa sprinkled some magic dust, and...

Trip landed on a doorstep!
A woman opened the door. Trip froze.
'Tim!' she called. 'There's a surprise for you!'

Tim ran to the door and squealed 'An elf!'

He rushed Trip inside, tore open the envelope and read out loud.

Tim whooped and whooshed Trip up onto the mantlepiece.

Trip sat very still all day.

Later, when Tim and his family had gone to bed, he tiptoed to the kitchen to find something to eat.

He spied a box of cereal on the countertop.
He just needed to find a way to reach it.
Trip found some tins and carefully built a tower.

Then he climbed...

He jumped... and landed head first in the box.
Trip was stuck!
Whoops!

That night, when all was quiet, Trip explored
the house. In the bathroom, he spotted
some toys and wanted a closer look.

Oh no! I messed up again, sighed Trip.

But the next morning, Tim roared with laughter. 'Mum! Look at Trip!' 'My goodness!' said Mum. 'What a cheeky elf!'

Cheeky? Trip puzzled.

That night, Trip remembered it was movie night back home in the North Pole.

Mmmm, popcorn!
His tummy rumbled.

Trip found the popcorn kernels and put the whole bag in the microwave.

Yummy! thought Trip, opening the door.

Popcorn exploded into the kitchen!
Trip was swept away in the tumbling avalanche
and buried in the salty heap.
Whoops!

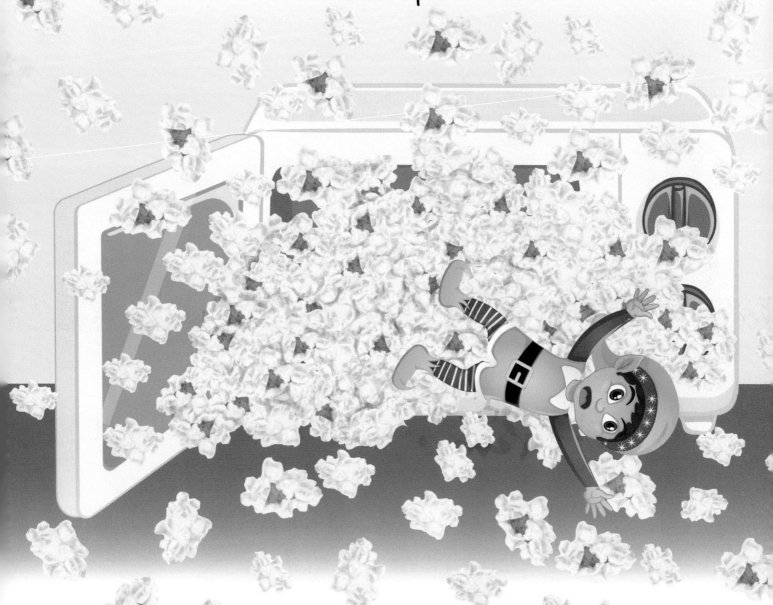

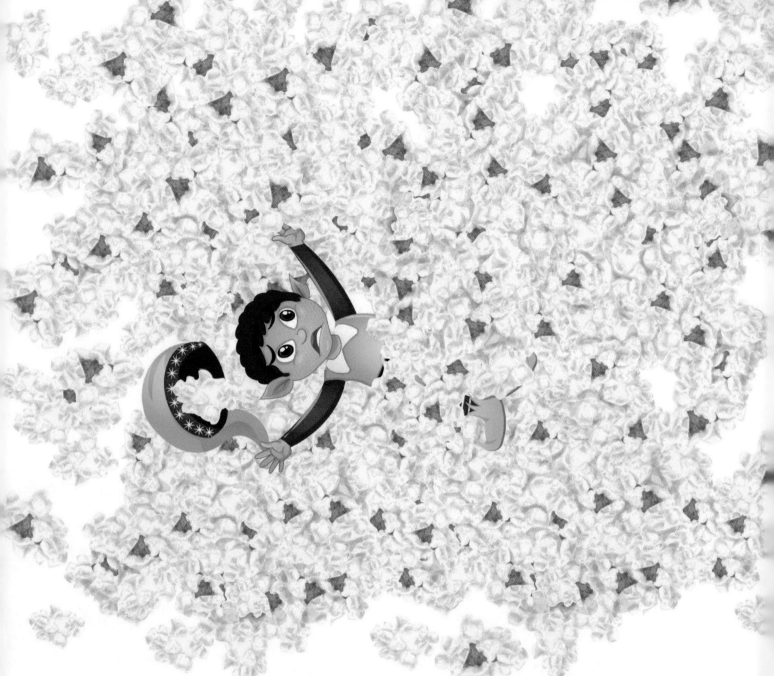

Oh no! Tim's bound to be cross this time, feared Trip.

But the next morning, Tim bellowed with laughter.
'My goodness!' said Mum.
'Trip's bonkers! I love him!' giggled Tim.
Trip felt overjoyed!

Night after night, Trip got caught up in one mishap after another. Each morning, Tim burst out laughing and even Mum couldn't help but enjoy their messy guest's visit. Trip began to relax and have fun.

On Christmas Eve, Tim laid out a mince pie for Santa and a carrot for Rudolph. He gave Trip the biggest hug goodbye and whispered 'Thank you Trip, this has been the best Christmas ever! I hope you visit again next year.'

When Santa arrived to deliver presents, Trip hopped in the sleigh. 'Santa! Santa! I'm not just a clumsy elf! I'm funny and cheeky and bonkers, and Tim loves me!' Santa nodded proudly, and Trip grinned from one pointy ear to the other.

Can you find 3 elves with red hats?

Trip would love to know
what you think of his book!

PLEASE LEAVE A REVIEW ON AMAZON!

How many stars do you give
The Clumsy Elf?

Printed in Great Britain
by Amazon

14164343R00020